STITCHED

#1: "The First Day of the Rest of her Life"

STITCHED

#1: "The First Day of the Rest of her Life"
Story by Mariah McCourt
Art by Aaron Alexovich

NEW YORK

STITCHED

STITCHED #1
"The First Day of the Rest of Her Life"

MARIAH McCOURT – Story
AARON ALEXOVICH – Art, Lettering and Cover
DREW RAUSCH – Color
SASHA KIMIATEK – Production Coordinator
MARIAH McCOURT – Editor
JEFF WHITMAN – Assistant Managing Editor
JIM SALICRUP
Editor-in-Chief

Charmz is an imprint of Papercutz.

ISBN HC: 978-1-62991-775-7
ISBN PB: 978-1-62991-774-0

Printed in China
May 2017

Charmz books may be purchased for business or promotional use.
For information on bulk purchases please contact Macmillan
Corporate and Premium Sales Department at
(800) 221-7945 x5442

Distributed by Macmillan
First CHARMZ Printing

STITCHED
CHARACTER BIOGRAPHIES

CRIMSON VOLANIA MULCH
Brand-new and brimming with curiosity, Crimson is a mystery even to herself. Made up of different girls, she doesn't know who she was, so how can she decide who she should be? Waking up in Assumption Cemetery is only the beginning, but she knows at least four things already: she has great hair, she loves animals, vampire boys are seriously pretty, and she definitely needs to find her selves. Whoever they were.

WISTERIA SMIALS
A shy werewolf who paints, Wisteria is a loyal friend with a soft, kind heart…but watch out. If you threaten those close to her or waste time bickering, Wisteria's inner wolf will come out. And it is not to be messed with. No one knows where she lives, which is a bit curious, even for Assumption.

SIMON
A swamp boy with a bioluminescent personality, Simon likes snacks, swimming, and Crimson. A lot. He lives in Assumption's swampy bayou and has no trouble saying what he thinks. He's determined and a bit overly confident, but he'll always be there for a friend.

QUINTON
Assumption's resident vampire boy, he's pretty, he's properly brooding, and he's more than a little stuck up. He's older than even he can remember and doesn't let much touch his undead heart. Until he meets Crimson and has to face a past he's not quite ready to deal with.

PARAMETER JONES
A "magical technician" with a prickly personality and more power than skills, Parameter is Assumption's only human resident. Well, only *living* human resident. Parameter is there to learn and practice magic and become the best. Just don't call her a witch.

CRUST
Half badger, half hedgehog, all cute. Crust is the perfect pet for Crimson and the most adorable undead companion ever made. Was she a gift from Crimson's mom? Does she like cupcakes? All she knows is that she loves Crimson and will follow her anywhere.

STiTCHED
1-3-16

QUINTON

SIMON

WISTERIA

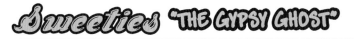

Sweeties "THE GYPSY GHOST"

Don't miss SWEETIES #1 "Cherry/Sky"! Available now!

Check out more in CHLOE #1 "The New Girl"! Available now!

not final art

Layouts for Ana and the Cosmic Race!

ART BY KATA KANE

Be sure to catch Ana and the Cosmic Race #1, on sale June 2017.

Welcome to

I am definitely obsessed with all things romance. It's fun, it's dramatic, and it's all about love. I think love is pretty amazing, don't you? When your heart beats faster at the sound of someone else's voice or the way they smile, you just feel more alive. And terrified! Or how about when just being around that special someone makes you feel like you're flying? Like you could do anything? Falling in love is one of the most incredible feelings, ever.

Of course, love is also complicated and painful sometimes. They don't call them "crushes" for nothing!

Yet, when I'm feeling kind of meh or sad, the first thing I want to do is read a romance. Maybe it's because everyone falls in love, has heartbreak and heartache. Maybe it's because there's really nothing like your first kiss. Whatever the reason, when I want to feel better, I pick up a romance and settle in. Usually with tea and chocolate, if I'm being totally honest.

Which brings us to Charmz, a new line of graphic novels just for you! With stories from all over the world, Charmz wants to celebrate love. Whether we're hanging out in Somerset, UK, the wilds of France, speeding through space, or waking up in a cemetery, love finds our characters and digs right in.

Whether you're in the mood for a (literally!) sweet tale about sisters, chocolate, and forbidden love, or exploring the mysterious darkness of Assumption Cemetery where vampires and swamp boys romance stitched girls, you'll find a lot to relate to.

My favorite kinds of romance are epic, sweeping, and probably just a little bit hilarious. As seriously as I take love, if you don't laugh a little at the things we'll do for it, well, you'll end up actually lovesick. Which is definitely something the girls in our books have to deal with from time to time. Not to mention fashion faux pas, weird chocolate recipes, ghosts, zombie sheep, and puzzles through time and space!

I've read a lot of romances and I definitely have my favorites. I think the one I would take on a desert island would have to be *Pride and Prejudice* by Jane Austen. I know, it's old, but it's so witty, and funny, and real. It's been adapted so many times but it always feels fresh and relevant. Anyone could be those characters. Me. You.

Aside from editing this line of graphic novels, I'm also writing one: STITCHED. This spooky little cemetery book with vampires, werewolves, swamp boys and stitched girls is very dear to me. It's the book I've always wanted to write, with spectacularly weird creatures, spooky adventures, and lots and lots of awkward, splendid, romance. Crimson Volania Mulch is my favorite kind of girl; complicated, smart, curious, kind...but a little bit preoccupied with her own problems. And way too judgmental. No one is perfect! And if I woke up only knowing my name in a strange place, I might be a little self-involved, too. I mean, just who is that pretty boy she meets on her first night "alive," and where is her mother? What does a badger/hedgehog actually eat? Do werewolves like cupcakes?

What I want Charmz to be for you is like the book equivalent of a hot chocolate; sweet, maybe a little dark sometimes, comforting, and made just for you. You can curl up with our tales, settle in, and enjoy falling in love with our characters just like they fall in love with each other.

Remember: stories matter, love is powerful, and there's nothing like a love story to make you feel alive.

–*Mariah McCourt*

Please write to me any time about Charmz! mariah@papercutz.com

I would love hear from you.

STAY IN TOUCH!

EMAIL: charmz@papercutz
WEB: www.papercutz.com
TWITTER: @papercutzgn
FACEBOOK: PAPERCUTZGRAPHICNOVELS
REGULAR MAIL: Charmz, 160 Broadway, Suite 700,
                 East Wing, New York, NY 10038